KT-539-504

Contents

Chapter One
Jinx's Itch

'That black and white cat
is as daft as a brush!'

Dad was looking out of
the sitting room window.

'Look at it!' he said. 'It's
rubbing up against that lamp
post like crazy! It must have
an itch to scratch.'

Dad turned his attention
back to his newspaper.

Tom and Daisy were at the window in a flash. They had a good idea which cat Dad was talking about.

Sure enough, it was Jinx.

The children knew that Jinx wasn't 'daft' at all. He was a remarkable cat. He could talk, for one thing. And it was Jinx who had shown them the magic street lamp.

One of the street lamps
on Genie Street, where
Tom and Daisy lived, was
as amazing as Jinx. If you
rubbed it in the right way,
magical things happened.

Daisy watched Jinx closely.
'Look!' she whispered to Tom.
'He's doing the special rub!
*Once up… once down… then
three times round and round…*'

13

Jinx finished his third circle round the lamp post. The children saw the street lamp blaze into life. A ball of purple light shot from the lamp and across the street.

'Did you see where it went?' whispered Daisy.

'Somewhere opposite the shops!' Tom hissed back. 'Come on – let's go!'

They hurried to the front door.

Chapter Two
A Parcel for Mr Chan

Tom and Daisy had just
stepped outside when they
heard a familiar voice.

'Hullo, hullo! Look out,
my young friends! Special
Delivery coming through!'

A man in a purple uniform
came zooming towards them
on rollerblades. He had a long
parcel tucked under one arm.

'It's Mr Mistry!' said Daisy in delight.

'Stand clear!' cried the little man. 'Can't stop, bless my ears!'

He tossed the parcel to Tom as he zoomed past. Then he was gone.

'Wow!' said Daisy. 'Talk about getting your skates on!'

Tom looked at the label on the parcel.

'It's for Mr Chan,' said Tom.

Mr Chan owned the garage at the end of Genie Street. He mended cars and vans. There was a car wash at his garage, too.

The children hurried to Chan's Autos – but there was no sign of Mr Chan anywhere.

Then Daisy gave a sudden gasp. 'Tom! *Look*!'

CHAN

MR T CHAN
CHAN's AUTOS
3 GENIE ST

Chapter Three
Buckle Up

The car wash machine was glowing purple.

'So *that*'s what the street lamp's magic hit!' cried Tom. 'Look! It's moving!'

The car wash's big shaggy rollers were beginning to turn – slowly at first, then faster and faster. They began to foam with purple froth.

Someone had left an old camper van at the garage for Mr Chan to mend. The van's doors suddenly sprang open. Tom and Daisy jumped back.

Jinx the cat was curled up on the front seat.

'Well?' he purred. 'Are you going to get in? Or just gawp?'

The children looked at each other. They scrambled into the front of the van.

The camper van's doors
slammed shut. Very slowly,
the van began to roll forwards.

'What's happening, Jinx?'
asked Tom.

Jinx licked a paw. He wiped
it lazily behind his right ear.

'Nothing to worry about,' he
purred. 'But I should buckle
up, all the same.'

The children quickly
fastened their seatbelts.

Somehow, the van was moving – straight towards the whirling car wash. It trundled a little further and was swallowed up by the foaming rollers.

For a few seconds, all Tom and Daisy could hear was the *shoosha-shoosha-shoosha* of the car wash. All they could see through the van's windows was purple froth.

Then the noise stopped, and the bubbles cleared.

Chapter Four
Blast Off!

'Where are we?' said Daisy.

The whole world had turned topsy-turvy. The camper van was pointing straight upwards. The windscreen was filled with a view of clear blue sky.

'Er… I know this sounds silly,' said Tom, 'but I *think* we're on a launch pad!'

The van's sunroof suddenly
slid open. Mr Chan clambered
through it. He wasn't wearing
his normal overalls. He seemed
just as surprised to see Tom
and Daisy as they were to
see him.

'Well, hello!' he cried.
'A crew! Now this *is* a nice
surprise! It can get quite
lonely up in space, you know!'

'Space?' said Daisy. 'So, we really are on a launch pad? You're going into outer space – in a *camper van*?'

Mr Chan wriggled on to the seat next to her.

'Don't you worry about the *S.S. Vantastic*!' he said. 'She's the finest rocketship in Lampland!'

He began fiddling with the van's controls. There seemed to be quite a few new ones.

Mr Chan fastened himself in. 'Everyone comfy?' he asked cheerily. 'Super!'

He flicked a switch.

'Launching in ten... nine... eight... seven... six...'

'No safety belt for *me*, then,' grumbled Jinx. He gripped the seat with his claws.

'... five... four... three...'

Tom and Daisy braced themselves.

'... two... one...

BLAST OFF!'

There was a roar of rocket engines. Tom and Daisy were pinned in their seats as the *S.S. Vantastic* shot into the sky.

The rocket-van climbed at an incredible speed. Its flaming engines left a white cloud trail across the blue sky.

Soon it had left the world far behind. Its engines shut down. It began to drift in the blackness of space.

Chapter Five
Noom-rock

'We're now in orbit, 2,000 kilometres above Lampland!' said Mr Chan. He took a packet of biscuits from the glove compartment. 'Anyone for a ginger nut?'

'The stars look beautiful from up here!' murmured Daisy.

'And look at the Moon!' said Tom. 'It's so… pink!'

'That's not the Moon,' purred Jinx. 'It's the *Noom*.'

'Oh. Right. I see,' said Tom – who didn't really. 'But why the pinky colour? What's it made of?'

'The Noom?' Jinx shook his head. 'Why, *rock*, of course!'

Tom felt a bit silly for asking. He turned back to the view – and thought he saw a dark shape move across it.

He shivered. No. It was nothing. Just his imagination.

'I've probably got some Noom-rock you can have, actually,' said Mr Chan cheerily. He dug around in his pockets. 'I've been there often enough! Ah – here we are!'

He handed something to each of the children.

The Noom-rock was pink and white, and it felt sticky. It had tiny red letters running through it.

Chapter Six
The Broken Star

Suddenly the van's horn sounded. A red light started flashing on the dashboard.

'We've arrived!' cried Mr Chan.

The children could see a small glassy ball floating in space.

'What's that?' asked Tom.

'That, my friend,' said Mr Chan, 'is why we're here! It's the heart of a star!'

'A star?' said Daisy. 'But shouldn't it be… shining?'

'Exactly!' cried Mr Chan. 'It isn't working!' His face clouded over. 'And I have a nasty hunch who – or rather *what* – put it out,' he muttered.

Before Daisy could ask what he meant, he began rooting about in the back of the van.

'Anyway, it's our mission to fix it!' he said. 'We'll need my starlighter! But where *is* the blasted thing?'

'What does it look like?' asked Daisy.

'It's sort of long,' said Mr Chan, still searching frantically. 'And thin.'

'*Ahem*!' Jinx cleared his throat.

'Got a hairball stuck?' asked Tom.

Jinx scowled. He was resting his paw on something.

It was the Special Delivery parcel. It was long and thin.

MR T.CHAN
CHAN'S AUTOS
3 GENIE ST

Tom quickly gave the parcel
to Mr Chan, who unwrapped it.

'A brand-new starlighter!'
he cried. 'Marvellous! Just
the job!'

He grabbed some space
helmets from the back of the
van. Daisy helped Jinx put
his on.

Mr Chan slid back the
sunroof. They climbed out
into deep space.

Chapter Seven
Snuffa Attack

Mr Chan pointed to the star.

'I'll need to get quite close!' he told Tom and Daisy. They got ready to push off from the rocket-van's roof.

Then suddenly something large and shadowy whooshed past them.

Tom shivered again. 'What was *that*?' he said.

A huge creature was floating nearby. It was watching them with alien eyes. It didn't look very friendly!

'I knew it!' cried Mr Chan. He looked very pale. 'It's a Snuffa! They've put out quite a few stars lately! They feed on light energy, you see! Among other things.'

'Er... *what* other things?' croaked Tom.

Mr Chan gulped. 'The odd space visitor... or two.'

'It's moving closer!' cried Daisy. 'It wants to eat *us*!'

Suddenly, a fiery white ball shot from behind the *S.S. Vantastic*. It streaked across the darkness, leaving a trail of light.

A shooting star!

The Snuffa's eyes fixed on it greedily. With a monstrous roar, it turned and raced away, chasing the star.

Chapter Eight
Down to Earth

'Phew!' said Tom. 'Now I know why they say shooting stars are lucky!'

'That *was* close!' said Mr Chan. He pulled himself together. 'But back to the mission! We have a star to fix!'

They drifted over to the heart of the star. Mr Chan reached out with his starlighter.

'Now would be a good time to close your eyes,' said Jinx.

There was an explosion of light as the star lit up. Even with their eyes shut, the children were dazzled by the glare.

Then almost as suddenly the light faded away.

'Oh dear!' said Daisy. 'Has it gone out again?' She opened her eyes.

Mr Chan wasn't there. Nor was Jinx. Nor were the stars, or the Noom, or the *S.S. Vantastic*.

Tom and Daisy were back outside Chan's Autos.

They looked at the rusty old camper van. They looked at the silent, still car wash.

Tom put his hand in his pocket. He pulled out the souvenir Mr Chan had given him.

Genuine Noom-rock.

Tom smiled at Daisy. She grinned back.

Together, they set off for home.

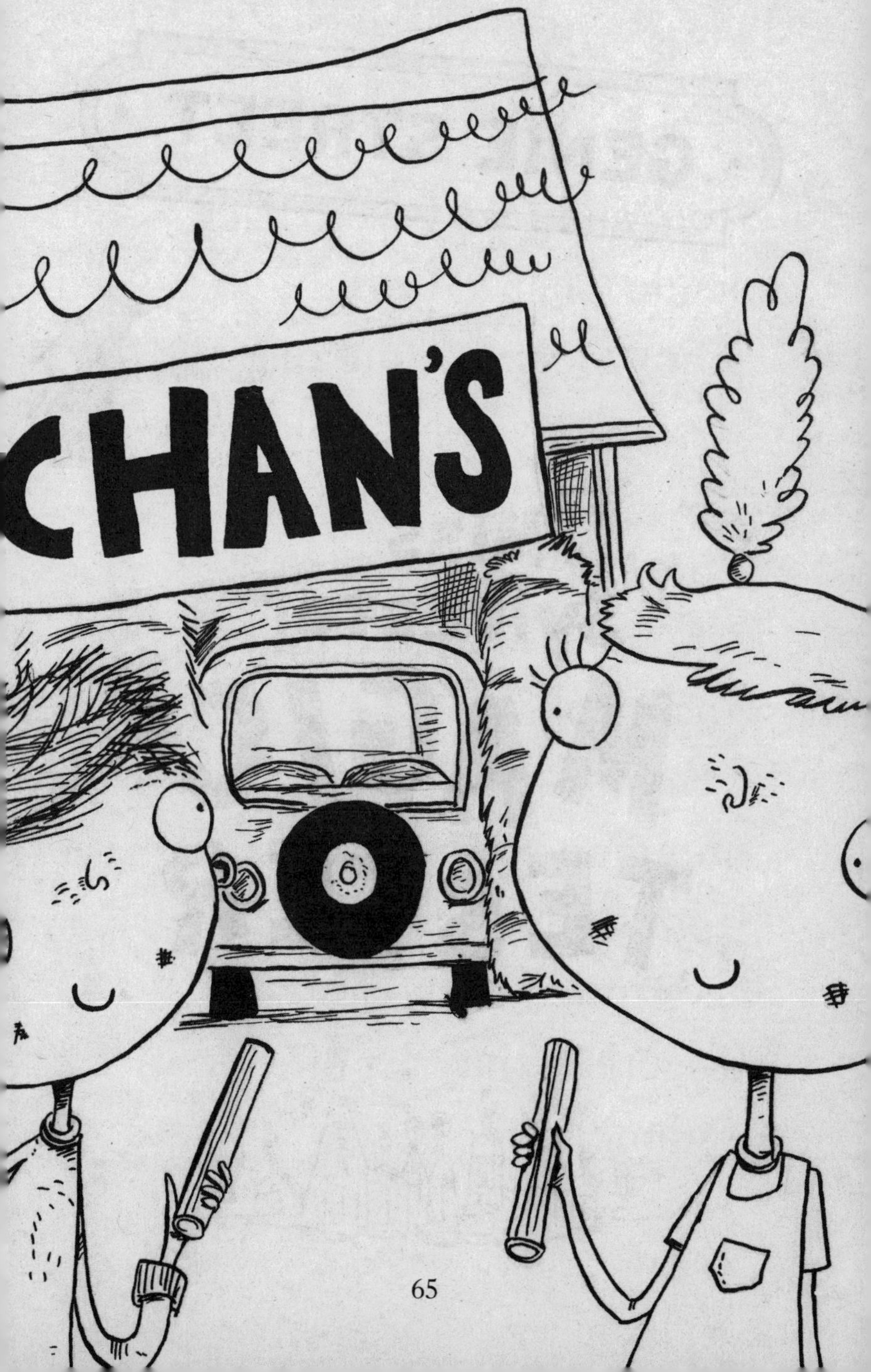
CHAN'S

· GENIE STREET ·

WARNING:
NEVER TRY
POTION-TESTING
AT HOME!

Miss Sylvester

MAGIC TESTER

Contents

Chapter One
A Cat Comes Calling

The doorbell rang.

Tom and Daisy were in the sitting room, playing Snap! Dad was in the kitchen. He had just started cooking tea. It smelled like one of his deadly curries. Mum was still at work.

'Can *you* get that, please?' yelled Dad.

'Okay!' Daisy called back.

Tom and Daisy went to the front door. There was nobody there.

Daisy was about to close the door, when –

'Ahem! Down here!' purred a rather cross voice.

'Oh, hello, Jinx!' said Tom. 'How did *you* ring the doorbell?'

'Never mind that,' said Jinx. 'You must come with me, right away. You're needed in Lampland!'

Tom and Daisy had visited Lampland before. A magic street lamp on their road had led them there. It was a secret, enchanted world.

'What do you mean, we're "needed"?' Daisy asked Jinx. 'How do you know?'

'Animal instinct,' said Jinx. 'I have a sixth sense. And a seventh. You need a few extras when you have nine lives. Now, come along!'

Jinx led them straight to the magic street lamp.

'I'll let you do the rubbing,' he purred. 'If it isn't too much trouble, that is. I've just washed, you see.'

'No problem!' said Tom.

He reached out to rub the lamp post with his hand.

'*Once up… once down…*' he chanted, '*then three times round and round…*'

Chapter Two
A Visit to the Chemist's

The magic street lamp lit up.
A ball of purple light burst
from it, and shot through the
air. It hit the door of the nearby
Green Cross Chemist's shop.

Tom and Daisy hurried to
look. Jinx prowled after them.

And then someone else
turned up, out of the blue –
BOI-YOI-YOING!

'Hullo, hullo!'

Tom and Daisy jumped in surprise. Mr Mistry had just landed right next to them. He was on a pogo stick. It was purple, to match his postman's uniform.

'Special Delivery for Miss Sylvester!' cried Mr Mistry.

Then – *BOI-YOI-YOING*! – he was gone again.

Tom laughed. 'Where did *he* spring from?' he said.

A tiny parcel lay on the pavement. Daisy picked it up. She read the label.

'It's for Miss Sylvester, at the chemist's,' Daisy told Tom.

'Come on, then!' said Tom. They exchanged excited looks. The magic street lamp had chosen this door. There was every chance it might lead to Lampland.

It was time to find out.

Chapter Three
The Woman with Green Spots

Tom and Daisy stepped through the glowing door. There was a flash of purple light. When it faded, the children's surroundings had changed completely.

They were in a large room. Its stone walls looked very old, like those of an ancient castle. It was some sort of laboratory.

'Look!' Tom hissed. 'I bet that's Miss Sylvester!'

Someone was busy at a wooden workbench. Tom had seen her before – behind the counter of the chemist's shop.

Miss Sylvester noticed them, too. She came over, smiling.

'Hello there!' she said. 'Where did you two pop up from?'

But Tom and Daisy were too busy staring to reply.

'You're covered in spots!' cried Daisy. A moment later, she realised how rude this sounded. But Miss Sylvester didn't seem upset.

'Well spotted!' she laughed. 'But don't worry! I caught them quite on purpose!'

Tom and Daisy looked puzzled.

'What do you mean, "caught" them?' said Daisy.

'And why would you *want* green spots?' said Tom.

'Because of what's happened to the princess, of course!' said Miss Sylvester.

The children looked blank.

'You *have* heard, haven't you?' she said. 'She is Princess of Lampland, after all…'

Tom and Daisy shook their heads.

'Well, I never!' cried Miss Sylvester. 'You're not from round here, are you?'

The children shook their heads again.

Chapter Four
The Cursed Princess

'Well, Princess Primula fell out with a sprite from the Fairy Forest,' said Miss Sylvester. 'The sprite cursed the poor girl. Now she's covered in spots!'

'How awful!' said Daisy.

'Quite!' said Miss Sylvester. 'So the king has offered a reward to whoever can come up with a magical cure.'

Miss Sylvester pointed to her workbench. It was crammed with bottles, flasks, tins and packets.

'Every witch and wizard in the land has tried to mix a cure,' she went on. 'It's my job to find out if any of them work. I'm the Royal Magic Tester, you see. Catching the curse myself seemed like the best way to start!'

Tom was staring at Daisy's face in horror. He looked at his own hands.

'It's quite easy to catch this spotty curse, isn't it?' he said.

'Ah, yes,' said Miss Sylvester, looking awkward. 'Sorry about that. I must have got a bit too close…' Then her face lit up. 'But now you can help with the testing, too, can't you?'

Chapter Five
A Dose of Magic

Miss Sylvester reached for a rack of equipment. She handed Tom and Daisy a strange double-ended spoon each.

'Magic-testing spoons,' she told them. 'You can try out a potion with *this* end. Then, to reverse its effects, just take a second dose with the *other* end. *Hey presto* – all back to normal!'

Tom went first. He chose a tall glass bottle with a fancy stopper. He poured out a spoonful of thick blue syrup and swallowed it.

It tasted peppery and made his eyes water. But that was all.

'That one didn't do much!' he spluttered.

Then suddenly his left leg began to grow.

'Help!' cried Tom. 'Make it stop!'

His leg was stretching at an alarming rate. Soon it was nearly five times its normal length. Then, just as his head was about to hit the stone ceiling, it stopped.

Miss Sylvester quickly fetched a stepladder. Daisy climbed up with the bottle of magic syrup.

A second spoonful of syrup, from the other end of Tom's testing spoon, did the trick. He quickly shrank back to his normal height.

'Well – *that*'s not the cure, then!' said Miss Sylvester. 'Let's try this one!'

She took the lid off a little silver tin. It was full of sparkly orange crystals. She offered them to Daisy.

Moments later, Tom was laughing his socks off.

'Well, I can't see your spots any more, Daisy!' he giggled.

It was true. A spoonful of the crystals had left Daisy with no sign of green spots. They were completely hidden by her new coat of thick orange fur.

Daisy quickly flipped her spoon and took another dose.

Chapter Six
Pesky Imps

And so the testing went on.
Tom, Daisy and Miss
Sylvester tried potion…
… after powder… after pill.
But none of the so-called
'cures' made the slightest
difference to their green spots.
'Maybe *this* one…' said Tom,
taking a spoonful of steaming
black gloop.

'Look!' cried Daisy. 'Your spots are changing!'

It was true. Tom's green spots were turning orange. Then they slowly went red.

'I feel like a set of traffic lights!' said Tom.

Now his spots were fading from red to pink. Soon they were almost the same colour as his skin. But then they stopped changing.

'That's almost it!' cried Miss Sylvester. 'It just needs a little boost! If I'm right, a tiny pinch of powdered Zingwort should do the trick!'

She hurried over to a cupboard that stood against one wall.

'Zingwort gives any magic a bit more oomph!' she said. 'I always keep some in here, just in case!'

Miss Sylvester opened the store cupboard door – and screamed.

'*Arrggh*!'

Three tiny green figures leapt out of the cupboard. They landed on the stone floor and scampered away across the laboratory.

Tom and Daisy had seen these little green creatures before. They were imps. And imps always meant trouble.

'The pesky little villains!' cried Miss Sylvester. 'They've been at my magical ingredients again!'

The imps had almost made it to the door. One had silver sparks coming out of its ears. Another kept burping orange bubbles. The third one's feet were flashing different colours as it ran.

Then they were gone.

Chapter Seven
Zingwort

Miss Sylvester took a tiny box from the store cupboard. Its lid was open. She held it upside down and sighed.

'The little terrors have had *all* my powdered Zingwort!'

The shape of the Zingwort box reminded Daisy of something.

'Oh! Miss Sylvester!' she cried. 'I forgot!'

Daisy handed over Mr
Mistry's Special Delivery
parcel.

Miss Sylvester opened it.
She was over the moon. It
was a full box of powdered
Zingwort.

She didn't waste any time.
She took a small pinch of
the yellow powder, added it
to the bottle of black potion
and gave it a good swirl.

Daisy and Tom both took a spoonful of the potion.

'It's working!' cried Miss Sylvester.

Within seconds, the children's spots had disappeared.

Miss Sylvester was very excited. 'We must take this cure to the king immediately!' she said.

But Tom didn't want to dash off *just* yet. There was something in Miss Sylvester's cupboard that he wanted to try out first…

WIZZO
EASY-
THROW
SNAP
CRACKE

Chapter Eight
Tinker Tom

Tom couldn't help himself.
He grabbed one of the tiny
Snap Crackers, and threw it
at the wall. He was expecting
a small 'bang' and a few sparks.

Instead, there was a huge
blast, an explosion of light
and a vast cloud of purple
smoke. The smoke slowly
cleared…

The children were back
on Genie Street.

Daisy gave Tom a look.

'Whoops!' he said. 'Sorry!'

'Never mind,' said Daisy.
'At least we left Miss Sylvester
with a cure for Princess Primula.
And we've still got these.' She
held out her magic-testing
spoon.

'Yeah,' grinned Tom. 'We
can use them for Dad's curry!'

Laughing, they headed
for home.

125

GENIE STREET

Here's what other children have to say about Genie Street and their favourite Lampland characters!

'This book is really good! I can't wait to read more Genie Street stories.' Callum, age 6

'I like the magic potions in *Miss Sylvester Magic Tester*. The best bit was when Daisy got covered in orange fur.' Henry, age 6

'Mr Chan Rocket Man and the children went into space and had an adventure, which was cool as I like space.'
Vincent, age 5

'I liked the talking cat Jinx. He is my favourite character. '
Amelia, age 5

'I like the way they always have a souvenir at the end of the story to remind them of their adventures.'
Sophia, age 7

Genie Street is a brand-new fiction series that
is the next step up from Ladybird's Read it yourself
Level 4. Ideal for newly independent Key Stage 1
readers, these books are for children who want
to read real fiction for the first time.

Collect all the titles in the series:

9781409312390

9781409312406

9781409312413

9781409312420

9781409312437

9781409312444

Each book contains two easy-to-read stories
that children will love. The stories include short
chapters, simple vocabulary and a clear layout
that will encourage and build confidence when reading.